Durga

THE DIVINE WARRIOR

Sukanya Basu Mallik

Ukiyoto Publishing

All global publishing rights are held by
Ukiyoto Publishing

Published in 2023

Content Copyright © Sukanya Basu Mallik

ISBN 9789358466591

In a time of darkness and despair,

The demon Mahishasura's tyranny knows no bounds. We need divine intervention!

And so, the supreme goddess Durga answered the call...

From the cosmic realm, a brilliant light emerged, as Goddess Durga descended to Earth. She is radiant and fierce with her mighty arms.

As Durga descended, her divine presence filled the hearts of the suffering with hope.

Mahisasura looked sternly as Durga emerged from the clouds.

I am the embodiment of strength and courage. Evil shall not prevail!

Durga fought the demons fiercely. Her sword cleaved through their ranks, her trident struck fear into their hearts and her arrows of light pierced through the darkness.

Mahisasura fought fearlessly against all odds eyeing Goddess Durga for the final kill.

Recognizing the threat, Durga summoned her lion companion.

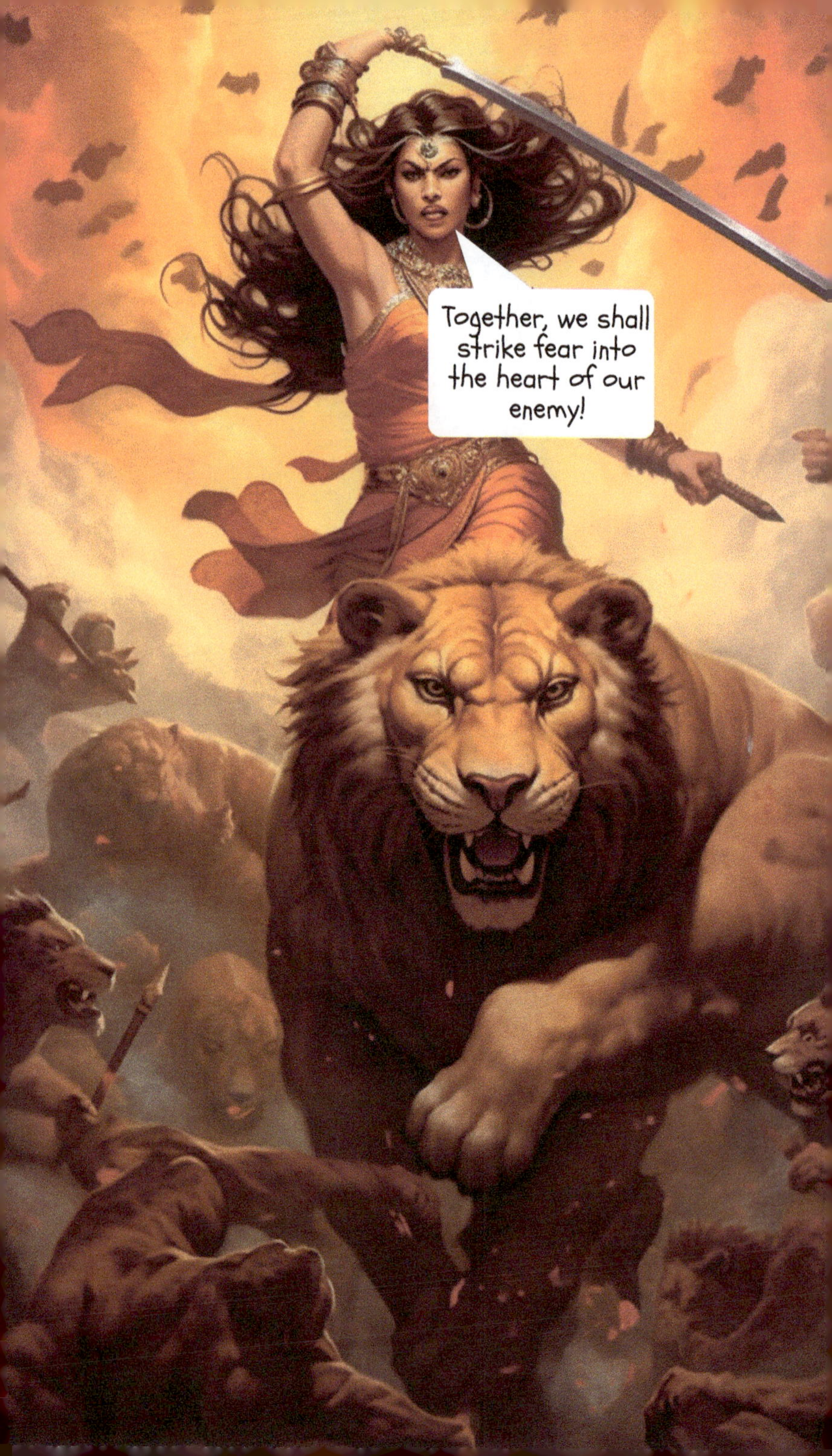
Together, we shall strike fear into the heart of our enemy!

The combined might of Durga and her lion companion turned the tide of battle.

Goddess Durga was surrounded by swirling energy and debris as she approached Mahisasura.

I will crush you, Goddess!

Mahisasura transformed into various powerful creatures trying to over power Goddess Durga.

Durga adapted to each of Mahishasura's forms, countering his attacks with her own grace and skill.

With every transformation, Durga adapted and matched her foe blow for blow.

With a mighty throw, Durga hurled her Sudarshana Chakra, severing the demon's form and bringing an end to his reign of terror.

Goddess Durga pierced her Trishul through the demon as he sent out his final cry.

The world rejoiced, liberated from the grasp of darkness.

All the Gods hailed Durga as the saviour of planet Earth.

Festivals were organized in Durga's honor, her story immortalized in the hearts of mortals.

Durga's legacy endured throughout the ages, her tales
passed down from generation to generation.

Goddess Durga's epic adventures continue to inspire and protect, reminding us of the indomitable spirit within.

www.ingramcontent.com/pod-product-compliance
Ingram Content Group UK Ltd.
Pitfield, Milton Keynes, MK11 3LW, UK
UKHW021302100625
6297UKWH00086B/812

9 789358 466591